HAMILTON'S HATS

First published 1996 as *Juice the Pig* by Macmillan Children's Books
Published 2007 as *Hamilton's Hats* by Macmillan Children's Books
This edition published 2013 by Macmillan Children's Books
a division of Macmillan Publishers Limited
20 New Wharf Road, London N1 9RR
Basingstoke and Oxford
Associated companies throughout the world
www.panmacmillan.com

ISBN: 978-1-4472-3491-3

Text copyright © Martine Oborne 1996, 2007
Illustrations copyright © Axel Scheffler 1996, 2007
Moral rights asserted

2 4 6 8 9 7 5 3 1

A CIP catalogue record for this book is available from the British Library.

Printed in China

HAMILTON'S HATS

Martine Oborne

Illustrated by Axel Scheffler

MACMILLAN CHILDREN'S BOOKS

Hamilton the Pig was very fond of hats. He had . .

big hats,   small hats,   tall hats,

floppy hats,   stripy hats,   feathery hats,

nd suitable-for-every-and-any-occasion sort of hats.

fact, he had so many hats that you would need
ore than all your fingers and toes to count them.

When Hamilton the Pig's mum saw Hamilton
messing about in his hats, she worried.
"Hamilton," she would say, "you are a very
vain little pig and I do not know what is to
become of you. You have many lessons to learn
in life and you will learn none of them from hats!"

But Hamilton did not listen. He was too busy

tipping

and cocking,

raising

and straightening,

and doing all the other things you do with hats.

One day, Hamilton the Pig was out and
about when he bumped into a giraffe.
Hamilton was wearing a tall, teetering,
high-as-a-chimney sort of hat. "My hat makes
me almost as tall as you!" he said to the giraffe.

The giraffe snorted and with one fell swoooop

snatched up the hat and flipped it onto her head.

"Mmmmm, indeed, a very fine hat," she said, ignoring the hot, cross piglet below. "I should like to keep it for myself."

"But if you are really determined to get your hat back, you must climb up my long, long neck to get it"

Hamilton looked up at the giraffe's long, long legs and her long, long neck.

It is not easy for little pigs to climb, but Hamilton did want his hat back and so he decided to do it.

was horrid. The giraffe
pt wriggling her neck
cause, she said,
amilton was so tickly.

But Hamilton was
determined and so,
at last, he got his hat.

"Wheeeee!" he cried as he slid down the back of
the giraffe's neck and bomped onto the ground.

'I am a very determined pig and I have my hat!''

The next day, Hamilton the Pig was out and about when he came across a crocodile.

Hamilton was wearing a fierce, pointy, snap-your-tail-off sort of hat. "My hat makes me almost as fierce as you!" he said to the crocodile.

The crocodile yawned

and, with a quick slurpety-slurp,

schnaffled the hat deep inside his mouth.

"Mmmmm, indeed, a very gobblesome hat. I should
ke to eat it for my dinner," drooled the crocodile,
gnoring the raging pink piglet. "But if you are really
rave enough to get your hat back, you must come
aside my hungry, hungry jaws to get it."

Hamilton looked at the crocodile's hungry, hungry jaws and his hungry, hungry smile.

It is not easy for little pigs to jump inside a crocodile's mouth, but Hamilton did want his hat back and so he decided to do it.

It was terrifying. The crocodile kept licking his lips because, he said, Hamilton was so tasty. But Hamilt was brave and so, at last, he got his hat.

Hurrah!" he shouted as he leapt off the crocodile's ongue and ran off as fast as he could. "I am a very etermined and brave pig and I have my hat!"

The next day, Hamilton the Pig was out and about when he met a band of monkeys. Hamilton was wearing a round, bouncy, let's-play-catch sort of hat. "My hat makes me almost as playful as you!" he said to the band of monkeys.

The monkeys laughed and, with a quick
flick of the tail, one monkey swiped the
hat and threw it to his friend.

"Mmmmm, indeed, a very fun hat. We should play with it every day," cried the monkeys, ignoring the angry piggy in the middle. "But, if you are patient, you can have it back when we are finished."

Hamilton watched the monkeys throw his hat high, high into the air. It is not easy for little pigs to be patient, but Hamilton did want his hat back and so he decided to do it.

Poor Hamilton. It was boring. The monkeys played for hours because, they said, it was such fun teasing Hamilton.

But Hamilton was patient and so, in the end, he got his hat.

"At last!" he sighed as he said goodbye to the monkeys and plodded off. "I am a very determined, brave and patient pig and I have my hat!"

The next day, it was cold. Hamilton the Pig was
out and about as usual when he spied a tiny mouse.
Hamilton was wearing a soft, teeny, let's-cuddle-up
sort of hat. "My hat makes me almost as small as
you!" he said to the mouse.

The tiny mouse sniffed and looked up at the hat.
A slow, miserable tear rolled down her cheek.
"What's the matter?" asked Hamilton.
"I'm cold and I have no house to live in. Your hat
looks so cuddly and warm. It would be just the
thing to curl up inside on a winter's night."

"ou want to sleep in my hat?" squealed
amilton, horrified.
Oh no," said the tiny mouse, "I could not possibly
k you to be so kind as to give me your hat."

Hamilton looked at the mouse as she limped unhappily away. It is not easy for little pigs to be generous and Hamilton did not want to give his hat away, but he decided to do it.

It was nice. The mouse kept shaking his hand and saying thank you because, she said, Hamilton was so kind. "Ah," said Hamilton, "I am a very determined, brave, patient and kind pig but I have no hat!"

So, happy, hungry and hatless, Hamilton the Pig
arrived home . . .

and set to work on a new and very special hat!